The Tale of Billy Bouncer

FOR NICHOLAS
Hoping you will do as well as Billy Bouncer
when you play for England.

The Tale of Billy Bouncer

Brian Johnston and Tony Hart

PELHAM BOOKS/Stephen Greene Press

PELHAM BOOKS/Stephen Greene Press

Published by the Penguin Group
27 Wrights Lane, London W8 5TZ, England
Viking Penguin, a division of Penguin Books USA Inc.,
375 Hudson Street, New York, New York 10014, USA
The Stephen Greene Press, Inc., 15 Muzzey Street, Lexington,
Massachusetts 02173, USA
Penguin Books Australia Ltd, Ringwood, Victoria, Australia
Penguin Books Canada Ltd, 2801 John Street, Markham, Ontario,
Canada L3R 1B4
Penguin Books (NZ) Ltd, 182–190 Wairau Road, Auckland 10,
New Zealand
Penguin Books Ltd, Registered Offices: Harmondsworth,
Middlesex, England

First published 1990
1 3 5 7 9 10 8 6 4 2

Copyright © Text Brian Johnston 1990
Illustrations Tony Hart 1990

Made and printed in Italy by L.E.G.O.

Typeset by Goodfellow & Egan, French's Mill, French's Road, Cambridge

A CIP catalogue record for this book is available from the
British Library.

ISBN 0 7207 1984 4

Mr and Mrs Bouncer lived in a box-like house on a shelf in Mr Spong's sports shop.

They were now elderly and worn out but they had two bouncing boys, Bob and Billy.

Bob was serious and well behaved.

Billy was lively, cheerful and mischievous.

They were both shining with good health and had bright red complexions.

During the day the two boys stayed in their house, hoping that some customer would buy them. They did not want to leave their Mum and Dad, but they were ambitious and wanted to play in International Cricket.

At night-time, after Mr Spong had shut up the shop, they would climb down from their shelf and play with all their young friends: Gerry Golf, Harry Hockey, Timothy Tennis and Freddie Football. They had lots of fun but were careful to climb back to their home before Mr Spong arrived in the morning.

One sunny June day a distinguished-looking man, in a panama hat, and wearing an MCC tie and blazer, entered the shop. He had a white moustache, side-whiskers and peered at Mr Spong through his monocle.

'I am Colonel Snodgrass,' he said, 'I am Secretary of MCC at Lord's and I want two new balls for the One-Day International against Australia tomorrow.'

'Please look round, sir,' Billy heard Mr Spong say, and secretly thought that Colonel Snodgrass already looked round!

The Colonel walked round the shop examining the various balls on display. The balls from Australia and India were jealous of the Bouncer boys, because the latter looked so shiny and well. They were also more expensive. So the Australians and Indians tried to catch the Colonel's eye by doing a jig and jumping up and down.

The Colonel was not impressed with their antics and told Mr Spong so.

'Have you nothing better than these?' he asked. 'We couldn't have them behaving like that at Lord's.'

Mr Spong pointed to the Bouncers' house, where Bob and Billy were sitting quite still, smiling at the Colonel.

'That's more like it,' he said, and picked Bob and Billy up and tossed them from hand to hand.

He seemed pleased. 'They look good, they feel good and are just the right size and weight. I'll take them. Please put their coats on as they will be travelling in the basket of my

bicycle.' (The Colonel was a mad-keen cyclist, and bicycled everywhere.)

Bob and Billy were thrilled at what the Colonel had said. They were going to Lord's to play for England. But they felt sad at leaving their Mum and Dad and kissed them a tearful goodbye, before Mr Spong wrapped them up in their coats.

Mr Spong placed them in the Colonel's basket. He was sorry to lose them. They had been good boys. But he was proud that they had been selected to play at Lord's.

Colonel Snodgrass set off for Lord's at a brisk pace, pedalling furiously and weaving his way in and out of the traffic until Bob and Billy felt quite sick. He was going so fast that a taxi driver shouted out to him, 'Steady, guv'nor, don't you know there's a 30 m.p.h. speed limit?'

Bob and Billy were not used to the roar of London's traffic and peeped out of the basket to see where all the noise came from. As they approached the Grace Gates at Lord's the Colonel slowed down, ringing his bell loudly.

An attendant sprang to attention, saluted, and opened the gates. The Colonel sped through and rode up to the back door of the Pavilion.

He took Bob and Billy up to the second floor and opened a door marked 'Players and Umpires only'.

They passed another door marked 'Dressing Room', and went down a passage with showers and baths on either side. Billy gave a slight shudder. He wasn't too keen on baths.

At the end of the passage the Colonel unlocked a door marked 'Umpires'. There was a small room with a table, cupboard, three chairs, a shower and a loo.

The Colonel put Bob and Billy into a drawer. It was to be their home for the night. They were both tired after their journey and all the excitement, and soon fell asleep.

In the morning they woke up to the sound of a lawn-mower and the rattle of milk bottles and hurrying feet. Nick Chase, the head groundsman, and his staff were busy preparing the pitch and the ground, and the caterers were arriving with all the food and drink.

The Bouncer boys pushed open their drawer and looked out. The sun was pouring through the window. It was a lovely sunny morning in St John's Wood.

Soon after 8 o'clock the door of the Umpires' Room was unlocked and in came two men. They were Dickie Bird and David Shepherd, the Umpires for the match. Mr Bird was small, perky and hopped around just like a bird. Mr Shepherd was larger and rounder, and moved more slowly. He had big rosy cheeks.

They chattered away, Mr Bird chirping about the possibility of rain or bad light stopping play. Mr Shepherd practised jumping up and down with both feet off the ground. He is famous for doing this whenever the scoreboard shows 111, 222, 333 etc. Billy longed to ask him *why* he did it. But he was too nervous and decided to keep quiet.

The Umpires started to make themselves a cup of tea. Dickie said to David, 'I'm afraid there's no soft sugar.'

'Oh dear,' said David, 'what shall I do?'

'Well, you'll have to lump it,' replied Dickie with a chuckle.

Billy started to giggle. Dickie heard him, and took him and Bob out of the drawer.

'They look two beauties,' said Dickie, 'let's give them their fitness test.' He then passed the two Bouncers through a gauge to see that they were the right size and shape. He also weighed them.

He patted the two brothers on the head. 'You'll do fine,' he said, 'but I must take you now to see the two Captains for their approval.'

They went first to the England dressing-room where the England players were arriving and unpacking their bags. The England Captain handled the two brothers and nodded his head with approval. He pointed to Billy and said, 'That one appears a lively sort of chap. I hope we can have him when we are in the field.'

Dickie then went along to the Australian dressing-room where their Captain had a quick look and said to Dickie, 'They'll be right, mate.' But before they could leave the room a large bad-tempered looking character, with a scowl on his face, rose from a seat in the corner. He had a big Mexican moustache, and a beard. He looked a nasty piece of work. He went up to Dickie. 'I'm Bruiser Bat,' he said, 'let's have a look at them.' He then took Billy in his huge hands and said, 'You miserable little squirt. Wait till I get at you out on the pitch, I'll

wipe that smile off your face. I'll batter you all round the ground until you are black and blue all over. So beware cobber.' And, so saying, tossed Billy contemptuously back to Dickie.

Billy tried not to look frightened but inwardly dreaded the moment he had to meet Bruiser out in the middle.

Back in the Umpires' Room Dickie put Bob in the pocket of his short white coat which was hanging up. He put Billy back in the drawer. He and David then went out on to the ground to supervise the preparation of the pitch.

Lord's had now become really alive. There was the sound of much chatter and old friends greeting each other.

Feet clattered up the stairs, as members hurried to get their seats on the two pavilion balconies. It was the start of a big day at Lord's, and Billy's heart beat faster at the thought of actually performing in front of such a large crowd.

Soon a tremendous cheer went up round the ground. The public address system had announced that England had won the toss and would bat first.

Dickie and David had put on their smart black trousers, white boots, short white coats and white caps.

The 15-minute warning bell was rung, and Billy felt disappointed that he would not be in action straight away. But at least he would not meet Bruiser Bat until later in the afternoon.

At 10.55 am Dickie and David left the room, locking the door after them. So Billy was left on his own, and decided to have a quiet nap.

He woke up about an hour later and heard roars of applause coming from the ground. He got out of the drawer and spotted a radio on the table. He had often seen Mr Spong listening to *Test Match Special*, so thought he would switch on and check what the score was.

He heard a voice say: 'I can see an 82 bus going down Wellington Road and there's a red bus, a blue bus and goodness me, I nearly said a blunderbuss! There's a thoughtful-looking pigeon flying past our box, a helicopter is hovering overhead and I can see a butterfly walking across the pitch – and what's more, it's got a limp! Oh, by the way, England have made a good start. After 20 overs they are 85 for 0. Gooch is 45 but was a bit lucky – he was dropped when 2. (Really, mothers should be more careful with their babies!) No, seriously, it was an easy catch and one that Bruiser Bat would have caught 99 times out of a thousand!'

Billy switched off. He sniffed a delicious smell coming through the window. It was of hot gravy and roast beef and, although he didn't know it, was coming down from Nancy's kitchen on the floor above.

Nancy was cooking one of her famous lunches for the players. Billy couldn't resist it. He knew he shouldn't but he got out of the window and climbed up the drainpipe. He looked through the window and there was the small, dynamic figure of Nancy with her lady helpers, carving meat, chopping vegetables and making puddings.

He tapped on the window. Nancy opened it and took him in. 'You poor wee thing,' she said, 'you look half-starved. Have one of these,' handing him a delicious brown bread beef sandwich. 'I was sending them up to Mr Johnston but I'll make him some more.'

Billy tucked in and Nancy said to him, 'Why not go up to the Commentary Box? It's just above on the top balcony. They might give you a piece of chocolate cake.'

She showed Billy the way and he went up the stairs to the balcony, making his way between the members' legs as they sat watching England bat.

He soon spotted a large white box. On the door was written: 'BBC *Test Match Special* – Please knock quietly' which Billy did. The door opened and Billy was nearly shot by a champagne cork which came flying out of the box.

Inside Billy saw the backs of four large men. One was smoking a big curly pipe with smoke oozing out of it. One with a beard was surrounded by books and was putting small dots on to a sheet of paper. Another was talking very fast into a microphone and the fourth, with a large nose, was munching a piece of chocolate cake.

He spotted Billy on the floor, picked him up and cut off a slice of the cake and gave it to Billy. Billy ate it gratefully and the man said, 'Are you enjoying it?' But Billy had his mouth full and when he tried to say. 'Yes, thank you,' he spat crumbs all over the box. Everyone laughed and someone offered him a glass of sparkling golden liquid which the commentators were sipping. But he shook his head as he realised he had a hard afternoon ahead of him.

Billy suddenly realised that the players were coming off for lunch and heard the commentator say that the England score was 143 for 3 off 36 overs.

Billy smiled his thanks to the *Test Match Special* team, and hopped his way down the stairs back to the Umpires' Room. He got there just as Dickie unlocked the door, and he scuttled in between his legs and climbed back into the drawer. Dickie and David were very hot and flopped

exhausted into their chairs. They were soon tucking in to some lunch sent down by Nancy.

While they were occupied Billy slipped out of the drawer and climbed on to the top of the table where his brother, Bob, was still inside the pocket of Dickie's coat. He looked tired but happy at taking three wickets. But he had lost his shine and looked a bit bruised where Gooch and Larkins had hit him for four's.

After half an hour's chat with Bob, Billy went back to his drawer, and Dickie and David put on their coats and went out of the room.

Billy was tired after his adventures, and soon went to sleep. He was woken up by the return of Bob and the Umpires. 'Not a bad score, 275 for 8. It will take some beating,' David said to Dickie. They only had five minutes between the innings before they had to go out again, and now had come the big moment in Billy's life. Dickie had taken him out of the drawer and put him in the pocket of his white coat.

Billy's heart was beating fast as he looked around the pocket at his new companions. There were two bails, six pebbles, a pair of scissors, some sticking plaster, a pocket knife and a small book marked: *Laws of Cricket*.

Billy peeped out. It was a real thrill to go through the famous Long Room with the members on their high stools, some of them already asleep.

Billy thought of all the famous cricketers who had once passed the same way, out of the door, down the steps and out on to the green grass through the little white gate.

There was a roar of applause from the crowd and Billy couldn't resist giving an acknowledging wave of his hand. He felt that at least some of the applause must be for him. Indeed he saw Mr Spong standing up and cheering in one of the stands – he had a white handkerchief, knotted at the four corners, on his head.

There was more tumultuous applause as the England team came out on to the field. Billy just couldn't wait to show what he could do to the Australians, and jumped out of Dickie's pocket with excitement.

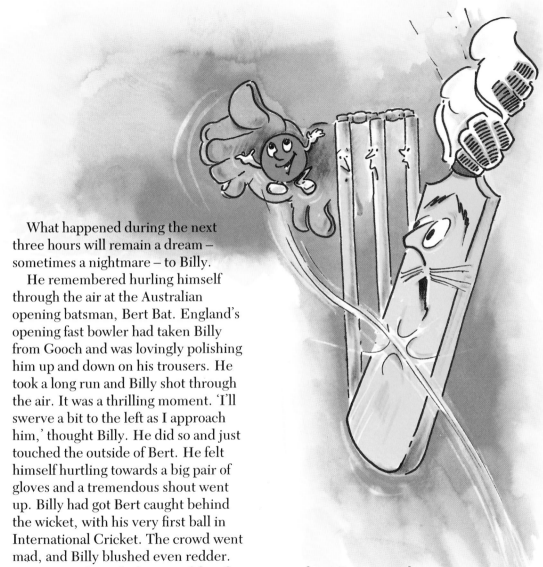

What happened during the next three hours will remain a dream — sometimes a nightmare — to Billy.

He remembered hurling himself through the air at the Australian opening batsman, Bert Bat. England's opening fast bowler had taken Billy from Gooch and was lovingly polishing him up and down on his trousers. He took a long run and Billy shot through the air. It was a thrilling moment. 'I'll swerve a bit to the left as I approach him,' thought Billy. He did so and just touched the outside of Bert. He felt himself hurtling towards a big pair of gloves and a tremendous shout went up. Billy had got Bert caught behind the wicket, with his very first ball in International Cricket. The crowd went mad, and Billy blushed even redder.

He went through the rest of the afternoon in a daze. Sometimes he went slower and twisted himself at the last moment so that the Bats missed Billy and were either stumped or bowled. He got hit for the occasional four but although the runs came quickly, wickets also fell.

Australia were 151 for 5 when down the Pavilion steps came the dreadful figure of Bruiser Bat. He glowered at the crowd, and as they booed him, he shook his fist and let out a maniacal cry.

There were 20 overs left and Australia still needed 125 to win.

Billy looked apprehensively at Bruiser as he approached the pitch. He shook his fist at Billy and called out, 'Come on, you pansy Pom, see what you can do.' Billy felt dreadful as indeed he might. Bruiser made a terrifying sight as he stood there in a menacing way.

The next forty-five minutes were a nightmare for Billy. Try as he might he could do nothing to stop Bruiser, who proceeded to hit him all over the ground. As Bruiser had said he would, he had battered poor Billy black and blue.

There was nothing Billy could do. He was in great pain where Bruiser kept hitting him. He was hot and exhausted and he realised that the crowd were no longer cheering him. They had gone silent as the Australian score crept up.

A roar went up as Bruiser reached his 50 with an enormous swipe. Billy twisted and turned but each time Bruiser gave him an almighty tonk and Billy was sent scuttling to the boundary. But he did manage to get two of the other Australians out so at least he had taken 7 wickets.

But Bruiser was still there, and with just one over to go Australia's score was 254 . . . 22 runs needed for victory.

Billy summoned up every ounce of strength from his tired little body. But it was no good. Bruiser hit him for 2, 4, 2, 4, and 4. The crowd were going mad. One ball to go. Six runs needed for victory and Bruiser's score was 94.

Billy was near to tears. Everything depended on him, and the crowd were cheering him on. He decided to hurl himself as fast as he could at Bruiser in one last attempt to get him out or at least stop him scoring a six. Bruiser stood at the crease challenging Billy to get him out.

54

NO 7 TOTAL NO 9
94 270 0
WICKETS 7
LAST PLAYER 2
NO 10 BOWLERS NO 11
HOW OUT B. 11

Billy approached Bruiser as fast as he could but he was so tired that instead of hurling himself at speed, he sailed up in the air. With a shout of triumph Bruiser swung at Billy and hit him high into the air. Billy was numb with pain. He felt himself sailing high over the Grandstand, just missing Father Time's scythe. Up and up he went over the stand, clean out of the ground and finally landed with a tremendous 'plop' in a gutter in Elm Tree Road.

Australia had won off the last ball, and Bruiser had made a brilliant hundred. Billy could hear the crowd shouting, the Australian voices louder than any. 'Good on yer sport. Well done cobber. Bully for Bruiser.'

All he could do was to lie there crying his eyes out. It wasn't just the pain. He had let England down. It was the unhappiest moment of his life.

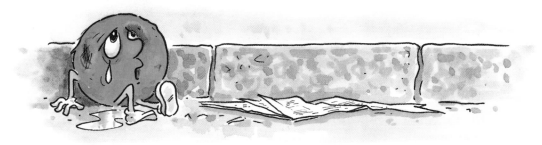

If he had not been crying so loudly he would have heard a tremendous counter-cheer from the England supporters, and loud booing from the Australians. What had happened was this: whilst David Shepherd signalled the six which gave Australia the victory, Dickie Bird, with his birdlike vision, had spotted a bail lying on the ground. Bruiser had hit his wicket and was out. England had won the match by 5 runs. Bruiser had made 94, and Billy had taken 8 wickets.

The crowd went mad, rushing across the ground to the Pavilion shouting, 'We want Billy, we want Billy.' All the England players came out on to the balcony. But the crowd were not satisfied. 'Billy, Billy,' they cried, and continued to do so for another hour whilst officials searched everywhere for him.

Billy knew nothing of all this. He was now covered by a piece of old newspaper, and lay in the gutter sobbing his heart out. He didn't know what to do or where to go. He could never look any cricketer in the face again. What would Mr Spong be thinking, and the Colonel too? He had let them down.

After a while the crowd dispersed and made their way home wondering what had happened to Billy.

As darkness fell a small boy, who lived in St John's Wood, was walking home after having supper with his granny.

His foot hit something and there was a yelp of pain. He had kicked Billy on one of his many bruises.

The small boy, who was called Nicholas, stopped and saw Billy curled up under the paper – his eyes wet with tears. He picked him up, rubbed him in his hands and put him carefully in his pocket.

Nicholas took Billy home and showed him to his Mum and Dad before taking him up to his room, where he put him under his pillow. They both fell fast asleep until the sun shining through the window woke them up.

Nicholas got up, washed and dressed and then took Billy into the garden where he threw him up in the air and caught him time after time. They both enjoyed it, and then Nicholas's Mum called them into breakfast.

Nicholas put Billy on the plate beside him and was busy eating his scrambled eggs when his father, who was reading the paper, said excitedly to Nicholas: 'I see we beat Australia off the last ball of the match. What a wonderful game, and the press are saying it was all due to Billy Bouncer who has mysteriously disappeared.'

Billy couldn't believe his ears. So he had not let England down, and he had got the better of that dreadful Bruiser. He danced around the table with joy. He was happy again, and he wanted to stay with his new friend for the rest of his days, just playing peacefully in the garden. He had had his big triumph and wanted no more crowds or excitement.

Mr Brown, Nicholas' father, wrote to Colonel Snodgrass and told him what had happened and that his son had found the missing hero. Could he please keep him and would it be possible for his brother Bob to come and join Billy?

Two days later there was a knock on the door, and there was Colonel Snodgrass holding Bob in his hand. He had cycled round from Lord's.

'Here's Bob, Mr Brown, and how nice to see you again Billy. We are all so proud of you and would like to make you an Honorary Life Member of Lord's. Whenever you want to come, ask Nicholas to bring you and Bob. You will always be welcome and we shall never forget Billy Bouncer's Match. Who knows, one day we may need you to win another game for England.'

The Colonel rode off and Nicholas, Billy and Bob went off hand in hand into the garden to play.